GHOSTING

written by
AMANDA DEIBERT

illustrated by
YANCEY LABAT

colored by **CARRIE STRACHAN**

lettered by **JANICE CHIANG**

GHOSTING

DC Super Hero Girls: Ghosting
Published by DC Comics.

DC Comics, 2900 West Alameda Ave., Burbank, CA 91505

Printed by LSC Communications, Crawfordsville, IN, USA. 7/30/21.
First Printing.
ISBN: 978-1-77950-765-5

PEFC Certified

This product is from sustainably managed forests and controlled sources

PEFC™
PEFC/29-31-337

www.pefc.org

Library of Congress Cataloging-in-Publication Data

Names: Deibert, Amanda, writer. | Labat, Yancey C., illustrator.
Title: Ghosting : a graphic novel / written by Amanda Deibert ; illustrate
by Yancey Labat.
Other titles: At head of title: DC super hero girls | DC super hero girls.
Description: Burbank, CA : DC Comics, [2021] | Series: DC super hero gir
| Audience: Ages 8-12 | Audience: Grades 4-6 | Summary: Diana Prince
used to being the best in everything in school, but to beat her foe sh
will have to rely on her friends to help her combat this newly danger
menace.
Identifiers: LCCN 2021020325 (print) | LCCN 2021020326 (ebook) | ISE
9781779507655 (paperback) | ISBN 9781779507662 (ebook)
Subjects: LCSH: Graphic novels. | CYAC: Graphic novels. |
Superheroes--Fiction. | Competition--Fiction. | High schools--Fiction. |
Schools--Fiction. | LCGFT: Superhero comics.
Classification: LCC PZ7.7.D4467 Dc 2021 (print) | LCC PZ7.7.D4467 (eb
| DDC 741.5/973--dc23
LC record available at https://lccn.loc.gov/2021020325
LC ebook record available at https://lccn.loc.gov/2021020326

chapter one

SWIIISH
Wonder Woman, behind you!
SWOOSH

Thanks, Katana! Glad to have you as my sister-in-arms!
When you ladies are done in the jungle, we could use some help over here in ancient Greece!
On our way, Zatanna!

Cheetah! These are sacred artifacts—I expected you to have more respect.
Oh, I do, Green Lantern! I'm just also counting on the fact that you'll use your energy to save them.
Hctaw taht top!
Oh wow, that's a great rendering of Zeus.
I'll make a snack out of you, Bumblebee.
You'll have to catch me first, and I'm pretty fast...
I hope.

Gosh, I hope this works... please, please, please.
Great work, Bumblebee! I am proud of your confident battle plan!
Oh, um, thanks. I was pretty sure it would work kinda.
DOLOS The Greek God of Trickery
Well, the good news is it looks like nothing was taken.
We should probably return all the artifacts to their rightful places.
Good thinking, Green Lantern. Supergirl and Batgirl can help you clean up while we take Cheetah to Metropolis PD.
Seriously?! Clean up duty? But...don't we have to get to school?
Wow, school? You must ***really*** hate clean up.

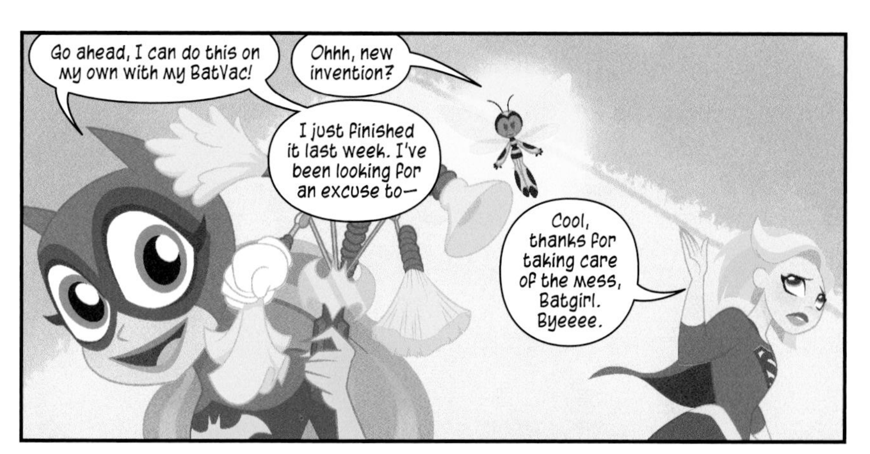
Go ahead, I can do this on my own with my BatVac!
Ohhh, new invention?
I just finished it last week. I've been looking for an excuse to—
Cool, thanks for taking care of the mess, Batgirl. Byeeee.

BRRRIIING!
METROPOLIS HIGH SCHOOL

LOVE
A-

And once again, I ask you all to look to Diana Prince as an example of what can happen when you apply yourself. I didn't even know it was possible to score a 170 percent on one of my tests.
Oh, but you did very well creating the test. I only found three errors in the section on ancient Greece.
I can't believe I rushed back for this.
A+

All right, team, tomorrow we've got a big match against Gotham High, so I want to see your A game.
THUD!

Well, that was very... moving, Doris. Thank you. And now, Barbara Ann, let's see if you can top that!

GO! HAMSTERS
Great work, Barbara Ann! And now, Diana!

Oh come on! How is that even fair?
Does it ever get exhausting showing everyone up?
Up where?! There is no one above me.
Yeah, we've **noticed.** Is there anything where you aren't the best?
Oh, of course! Tatsu and I usually tie when it comes to fencing. Right, Tatsu?
It is my great honor to occasionally best you, Diana.

CLINK, CLINK.
Shall we?
Are you girls done yet?!
Come on, fencing practice should have ended four hours ago!

Ha! You are distracted!

Ha ha ha! We are so alike. I admire your cunning.
Ha ha! And I, yours.

Okay, okay you are both amazing, whatever! I've been waiting here all afternoon to tell you something very exciting.
We're finally increasing our training schedule to twelve hours a day?!
No, something actually exciting.
What is your news, Barbara?

I'm having a slumber party on Saturday! And I know it's going to be Tatsu's first ever which is why it will be epic! There's even a theme.
Ohhh, a Tatsu's theme with swordplay is most excellent!

Well, actually, since it's at my house the theme is kinda gonna be Baturday Night Fever.

I don't get it, Babs.
Bat-urday... like Saturday...but Batgirl style?
Never mind. It's gonna be awesome. We'll play games, have snacks and Tatsu will be totally initiated into our girl time!

And no... training?
That's the best part!
Best?!
No time for that, there's been a break-in!
BEEP! BEEP! BEEP!
Here at school?
Seriously, who breaks into a history classroom?

Whatever's on that thumb drive, you are not about to get away with it, Cheetah. You're surrounded.
Yes, release the driving thumbs!
Ha! You'll have to catch me first!

COUGH!
COUGH!
COUGH!

I've got you!
Oh? Do you?

BAM!

But how did you—? You were just—?! I had you!

I'll knock the spots right off you!

More like you'll be seeing spots. Ha ha ha! Rawwwr!

Tuo nrad tops!

POOF
Ta da!

What? Weren't expecting an encore performance?

OOOF!

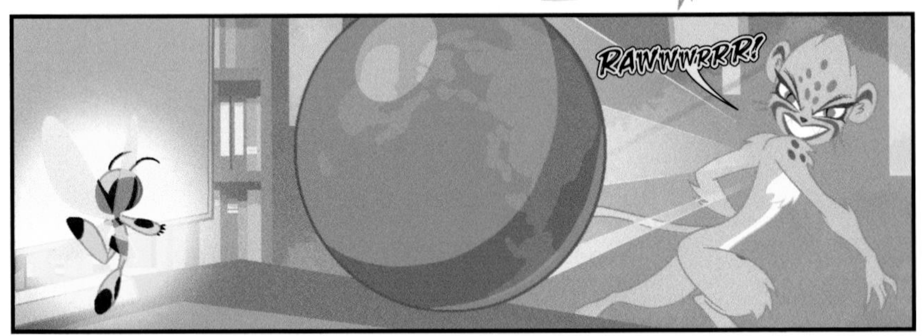

RAWWWRRR!

Globes? Why did it have to be a globe?

I've got you, Bumblebee!

And I've got you!
Wait! You were just over there?!

CLINK!

Give up now and at least you will keep your dignity.

I've got your back, Katana!

Seems more like I've got **your** back, Wonder Woman!

But...I had her?

First, we shall tend to our wounds with frozen deliciousness...and then we will strategize and see where my leadership has failed us in defeating our foe.
Sweet JUSTICE
She was a worthy opponent.
I just don't understand how she beat us so easily.

Yeah, it was almost like...she was everywhere at once.

Don't beat yourself up, Wonder Woman.
But I didn't beat myself! Cheetah did!

Oh, Wondy... let's just get you a sundae.
SLAP!

chapter two

Ah, yes, nothing like the freeze of the brain to put things into perspective! Another day is tomorrow!
And we'll totally figure out how to stop Cheetah.
Yes, I think tomorrow will be brighter for sure.

One brighter tomorrow morning...
Wow, the sun is actually brighter. How did you know that, Karen?
I watch the Weather Channel.

Why?! To put you to sleep?
To decide what to wear?
No, in the morning for excitement! Nothing pumps me up like tracking atmospheric conditions.
No time for talking small, ladies. I must hurry to class. I am always the first student to arrive in time to feed the class newt!

Here you go, Sir Isaac.
Oh...hello, Barbara Ann.

Looks like someone finally beat you to class in time to get a turn, Diana.
Well, yes, it does seem fair that I should allow others a chance to enjoy giving Sir Isaac his sustenance.

Time for a pop quiz with a speed bonus! The first person finished with all of the correct answers gets ten bonus points.

Oh this will be a piece of—
Done!
POP QUIZ
1. Who is the Greek god of war?
2. Who is the Greek goddess of the hunt?
3. Who is the Greek god of the ocean?

These are all correct! Barbara Ann, I'm very impressed.

Looks like there might be a new top of class.
That was an impressive show of brainpower and speed. You have my respect.

Good luck, Diana!
She doesn't need luck. She has skills.

TWEEEEEET!

Way to go!
GO! HAMSTER

Oh...good race, Barbara Ann.

Okay, time for a talk of the peps, Diana.
It is an honor to strive against those who best you.
It will make you a wiser student and a stronger warrior.
And if you bring shame upon Themyscira, your mother will ground you to the island for life...

Good news, Prince. Half the opposing team didn'tshow up.
You've got this gymnastics meet in the bag...not that you needed no-shows to do it.
I prefer winning fairly, but I shall still put the better of my feet forward.

Are you okay?
Sure. Let's just...get my next defeat over with.

Come on, Diana! It's not fun if it is not a challenge.
Then perhaps you should find a more worthy opponent.

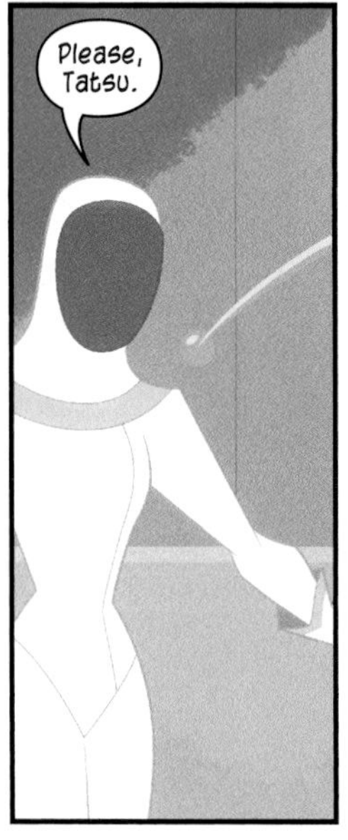
Please, Tatsu.

And the winner is Tatsu Yamashiro!

What's wrong?
Shouldn't you be basking in the glory of victory?

It's pretty empty when you don't make me work for it.
I'm sorry. I just...it is truly an honor to fight against people who are more skilled than I am, but this just feels...

I agree. Something is wrong. It is unlike you to fall behind so consistently.
Maybe I'm not training enough. Yes, that's it!

No, Diana, I am not saying it is your fault. Some things are beyond our control—
Exactly! I need more self-control!
Text the girls, Tatsu—we are going into training overtime!

Must...train harder.
38th FLOOR

90th FLOOR
Ah, that was a nice warm-up.

That...was =wheeze= the warm =gasp= up?
Yes, and you look quite warm, Batgirl.
We shall train until we are all in premium fighting shape.

I mean, I just lifted an entire bus off the freeway yesterday, so I'm feeling pretty tip-top.
LEX

Your tips can always be topped. Now let's see some sweat, ladies!

567... 568—
Do you think we could get some sleep soon? I'm volunteering at the animal shelter in the morning...
Sure, just a few cooldown laps around entire city and we're done!

HAVE YOU SEEN DORIS?
Yawn

How are you =yawn= doing this?
Good Morning, Jessica!
It is important to push ourselves to the limit. We'll do another twenty miles with all of the Super Hero Girls right before school.

Oh, okay... see you then.

I took it upon myself to do a few extra-credit essays.
But...you already have an average of 121 in this class.

It's worse than I feared!

Karen, I have **never** had bags under my eyes before. This training has to calm down.
I ≑yawn≑ agree it's a little much.

And I mean, look at this...my arms are almost too sore for me to do magic with a flourish...
Teg eht skoob!

See?
Karen! Zee! Get those knees up.
This is valuable time between classes that you could use to up your training!
PLOP!
Oh, looks like I gotta run...so that I don't have to run.
Yzal!
Oh um, sure, Diana.

Beckett Jackson?
No? Okay, Garth Bernstein?
Here!
Max Alexander?
Karen Beecher?
Here...barely.

Hallie Isler?
Hallie?
Where is everyone today?
ZZZZZZZZZZZ...
And could the students who *are* actually here please stay awake?
The square root of two is 1.41421356237!
That's lovely, Ms. Beecher, but this is English class.

The school day is over! Let's get training!

Okay, that's enough for me.
I know, right? This is exhausting.
Oh, I'm not exhausted, but I am *so bored!*

chapter three

LAZARUS
FOOD
TICKETS
LAZARUS PIT
That's more like it.
Just make sure you make it back in time for Baturday Night Fever!
KITTY RIOT
BLUNDIE
Heart of Sass
LIVE
Sweet!
ZZAP!
BLUNDIE
Heart of Sass
LIVE
Livewire!
Supergirl, how electrifying to see you.

Ahhhhh!

AHAHAHAHAHAHA! Thanks for the boost, Supergirl. I hope you're hungry, because I'm about to serve deep-fried Kryptonian!
ZAPPPP!

Do what you want to me but I'm not gonna let you wreck the Lazarus Pit.
I'm going to that Blundie concert one way or another.

Wait, you like Blundie?
No. I *love* Blundie.

Heart of Sass
Really? Me too!
Do you...I mean, what if we put this whole fight on pause until after the concert next week? I was just coming here to buy tickets anyway.

I actually have an extra one. Giganta totally ghosted on me this week and it's a whole thing...
Wanna be my plus-one?
Oh, wow, really?! Like... friends?

Well, more like temporary punk rock truce. But yeah, when it comes to Blundie you can call me anytime.
ZAP!
I've got a slumber party to catch.

Welcome to Baturday Night Fever! Tatsu's first-ever slumber party!
The only dancing I am willing to do is with my sword.
I am sure the theme of Bat-humans doing 70s dances is a very normal teen tradition in the world of man.
Nope. It's just Babs being Babs.
Let's play truth or dare—with Diana's lasso!
Ohh, I do like the sound of something daring!
Truth or dare, Zee?
Truth!
Who do you have a crush on?
Myself, obviously. I'm the most attractive person at school.

Truth or dare, Kara?
I'm only interested in food-related dares.
Ohhh, I dare you to go get us some vegan hot dogs!
Awww...I really walked into that one.

Your turn, Diana! Truth or dare?
Oh well, truth is kind of my thing so...

Although, I should also be daring and bold, so perhaps a dare...
But if I choose that, does it mean I have lost the core of what I stand for...
Is that why I am losing my footing? Or is it because I am becoming less brave?
Which is the right choice?

Diana, it is a game. Just go with your gut.
But I fear I have lost my guts! And if I cannot find my guts how do I know who I really am?

Uh, could you lighten up on the gut talk? I just ate a **ton** of vegan dogs.
Ohh! Yum!

I am sorry to be the pooper on the party—
Awww, come on! No gross talk.

I need to go do some more training.
I'll come with you!

I am daring...
CLANG!

I stand for truth...
I—
OOOF!

I do not stand at all.
You're distracted, Wonder Woman. Stop letting this get into your head. You've got this.
And you're not alone.

You know, it's okay to have hard days. We all do.
I mean, my entire suit was an accident, but it turned out to be a pretty good thing in the end.
What you need to do is to get out of your head. I never think before I act and it ***always*** works out for me. Watch!
Batgirl, throw something.

ZZZZZIP
See? Just don't think.

That was my favorite batarang! It took me weeks to make.
Okay...it works out most of the time.

What Supergirl is trying to say is that you need a little break.
And there's no better break than a night on the town!

I do not understand how this helps my training?
It won't. We're here to get your mind off that.
Ha! In a few minutes you won't even remember your name.
Missing

You may be my dearest friends, but I will not allow you to wipe my memory.
Oh, I can't wait to tell her!
No, Diana. But you will probably get a little giddy—
We called Steve Trevor and he's meeting you here for a date
SQUEE!
A date? Here? NOW?! Oh no, no, no, no, no. I am in NO condition to do that.
Which is exactly why you must. You've been working so hard for truth and for honor.
It is time for you to put that aside and focus on the most powerful thing of all...
Love!
Amore!

He said he'd be here in fifteen minutes. Just enough time for us to dash. Have fun!
Wait, you are leaving me here...alone?!

Oh no, Diana, you won't be alone. Steve will be here to join you for what I hope will be a delicious vegan meal. Bye!

Tatsu, please.
Well, I could wait with you until he gets here. Maybe we could do a little more training?

Absolutely not. The whole point of this is to give us all a break.
Everyone is leaving and Diana will enjoy the teen custom of a typical awkward date who sweats too much.

Stay with me, Babs, you're my only hope.
Sorry, Di. I'm headed to the arcade. They've got a new VR game where it's like you are actually driving the Batmobile. I can't wait!

chapter four

Can I get you something, Miss?
No thank you. I am waiting for a date.

SMOOCH

Oh carbs, thank you for a lovely evening.

Diana!
OLIV
QUE

Oh. Hey, Babs.
Where's lover boy?
OLIVER QUEEN
I guess he had something else to do.

But we texted him just before we got here! I can't believe he ghosted.

A ghost?! Where?
Come forth, you undead spirit, and I will send you to your final resting place!
No, no— ghosted. It's just when someone bails on you without telling you why.

So it is one of those speech figures?
Yeah, no actual ghost this time...unless you mean the ghost of human decency.
Steve Trevor is in the doghouse big time.

Nope. Not an actual doghouse either.
Ghosts living in dog shelters... the world of man has such odd speech figures.

Come on, Livewire...if I miss this show you are **seriously** gonna be in the doghouse.
TICKETS
BLUNDIE
Heart of Sass
LIVE

BLUNDIE
Heart of Sass
LIVE
TICKETS
=Sigh.=

BLUNDIE
Heart of Sass
LIVE
TICKETS
This is what I get for trusting a super-villain for concert tickets. Guess I gotta figure something else out.

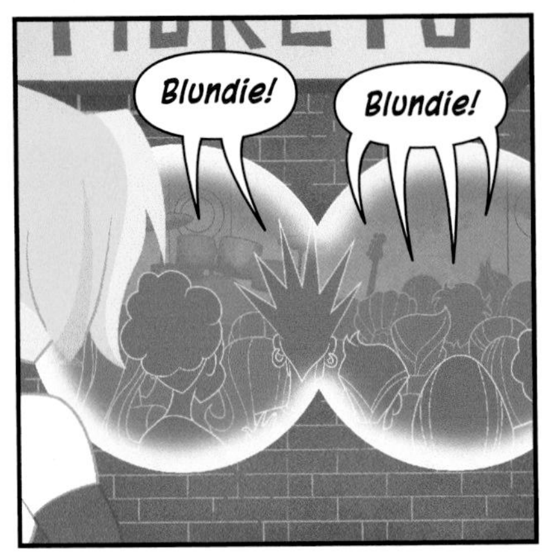
Blundie!
Blundie!

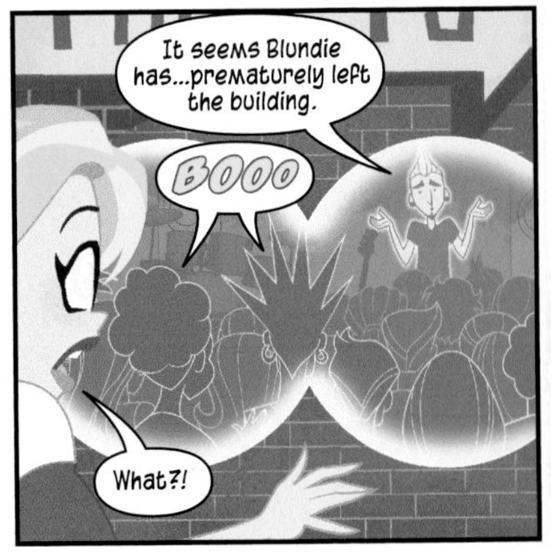
It seems Blundie has...prematurely left the building.
BOOO
What?!

Finally, a chance to relax and do my favorite thing...study with my study buddy.

5:00

GARTH

Garth, where r u? Library closes in an hour!

You can study anytime you'd like, but you can't stay here.
But my friend—
I had imaginary friends too and I turned out just fine, dear.

THE AMAZING
ZATARA DUO!
For our next act—

My incredible daughter, Zee Zatara, will make me disappear.

Ta da!

And now my father will reappear!

Uh, Dad?

Dad!

Ta-da! Look how thoroughly he vanished!

There will be no encore! Thank you!

Hal is usually a little late, but this is an insult to Lantern Corps training.
It's beyond even his gigantic ego...
Do you think something is wrong?
Yes. Yes, I do.

Hey, Barry, have you seen Hal around?
Nope. Honestly, I haven't seen many people.

Can I get you something?
Oh, nothing yet, just gonna meet some friends.

Society is full of rude ghosts! It must be stopped!
Oh no, did I miss a new super-villain?
Yeah, Steve Trevor.

He's a villain?!
Worse. He stood Diana up.

Oh no...he ghosted?!
Exactly.

Yeah well, he's not the only one. Livewire bailed on our plans too.
Wait...you had a date with Livewire? As in... our nemesis?!

She had an extra Blundie ticket.

We have a much bigger problem here!
Bigger than missing Blundie?!

Um, *yeah.* My father still hasn't reappeared. I've tried every incantation I can think of...
Latnerap ecnadiug!

See?!

And I can't find Garth anywhere.

Hal Jordan is missing too.
I ♡ MAC
Oh great. It's a whole *town* full of rude ghosts.

Unless it's not them.

chapter five

What's your theory?
I'm not entirely sure yet. It's just too big a coincidence.
Something sinister is happening.

Well, I mean...something like this has happened before. I still have nightmares from the time you used the Soultaker to remove our souls from our bodies.

You think it's *me?!*

I am sure that is not what Kara is implying at all, Tatsu.
Yeah, for one thing if you'd used the Soultaker there'd be soul-less bodies littered all over Metropolis.

Oh gosh, sorry, I didn't mean that in a bad way! I mean, yes, lifeless bodies are bad, but I was just stating empirical evidence and...
Wow, I should just stop talking.

Whoa, whoa, whoa, Tatsu, I **do not** think you did this. I just agree this feels supernatural.
I'm still deeply sorry for that whole uh...incident.
We've been through worse.

We won't be able to catch the actual person responsible if our shapes are not on the top of our tips.
Back to work!
Diana, shouldn't we take a moment to really think about—

We train.

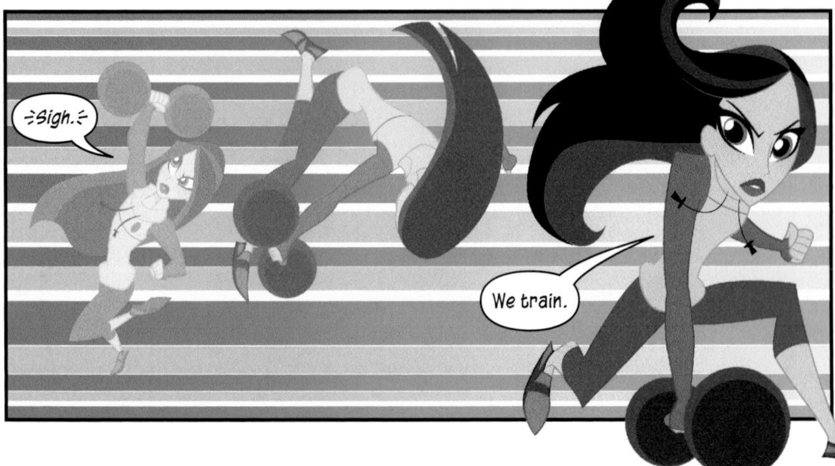
=Sigh.=
We train.

Ben? Lexie?
This is sooooo annoying. Where did everyone go?
Rehtaf latrop!
Dad?! Are you there?
Seriously, stop messing around.
Your friends are missing?
They were *just* here.
I'll help you look.
No, it's fine. I'm sure they just ghosted. People are so rude.
Help! Robbers!

Stop, thief!
She stole all the jewelry!
Don't worry—she's not the only one with cat-like reflexes.
JEWELRY

I'm im-purrr-essed you can keep up.
That's not all I can do.

My *jewels!*

Wonder Woman, get the jewels back to the shop. I'll deal with the feline.
The shop owner said there were security guards right outside the door but now they're gone.
Catwoman, what did you do to them?
Don't look at me. I just happened to be on the prowl.

They aren't showing up anywhere on my tracking device. They've just... vanished.
They aren't the only ones.

Wow, she is *slick.*

It just doesn't add up. It isn't easy to escape the Soultaker.

I'd love nothing more than to come up with elaborate conspiracy theories about how and why this happened, but that would make me late for my shift at the Burrito Bucket.
BEEP! BEEP!
Anyone hungry?

Dad nruter!
≑Sigh.≑
Barbara, how many times have I told you the napkins should be dispensed from right to left and not left to right?! This is the Burrito Bucket, not the Burrito Barn.
≑Sigh.≑

That seems like an ineffectual managerial style.
You're tellin' me.
This burrito fold is unacceptable! The angle of the crease is all wrong.

Hey!
Make this customer a new burrito, Gordon!

Mr. O'Shaughnessy should be taught a lesson.

BURRP!
It's not gonna be by me. His burritos are too delicious.
Are you coming, Tatsu?
I'll be right there.

Who are you? Did the Burger Prince send you?!

You need to learn to treat your employees better...or I'll have to teach you some respect.
Whatever you want! Just please don't hurt me.

What was that?

Gordon, that drink machine had better be clean!

Mr. O'Shaughnessy?!

Has anyone seen Mr. O'Shaughnessy?! The lunch shift is over, but I can't leave without checking with him first or I'll be fired—and I can't find him anywhere.

Did you check the uh... restrooms?

I didn't go inside but I yelled. Very loudly.

This is impossible. He's just gone.
I've tried multiple spells, but it's just like my dad. Not a trace.
PICK UP

Who was the last person to see him?
I don't know— he just went to his break room and—
It was I.

I had a chat with him about respect.
PICK UP

And thennnnnn?

chapter six

And then nothing. When I left he was still sitting at his desk.

I know how bad this looks. I won't lie. I did threaten him, but I didn't harm him. I just wanted Babs to be treated the way she deserves.
You've been such a nice friend to me. You threw a slumber party for me...which I left.

I was the last person to see him...and the last person to see Catwoman...I know it looks bad.
I've harmed people in the past...including all of you, but—

We know you didn't do this, Tatsu.

PICKUP
You do?

Yeah, if you were evil I'm pretty sure we'd have noticed by now.
And you only left Bab's non-sleeping party because you were worried about me.
Thank you so much. I was sure after you looked at all the evidence you'd want me to leave the Super Hero Girls.

No, we need to analyze this evidence and figure out what actually is happening.
If I were in top form, I would know what was happening. We should train.
Not this again. Diana, you're fine. Wonder Woman is still the best of the—
Wonder Woman?! Where?!

Ohhh, Wonder Woman isn't here. That's just the name of our new to-go special.
If you order a Wonder Woman burrito and eat it anywhere but here, it's on the house.
Wow, really?

Yep. Okay, have a great day.
Bye!

SORRY, POWER'S OUT!
Sorry we're CLOSED

Okay, I can't leave until we find Mr. O'Shaughnessy, but we need a plan before I accept any more customers.

Don't suggest training again! It's time to act. I'm going out there.
I'm with Kara. Every second we aren't doing something is...
A second I could be finding my father.

Emotions are high. We are all missing people. Now is the time to work together. We need to pause and meditate.

OMMMM...
If I were an overly meticulous and critical manager where would I beeeeeee...

Wait! If the Soultaker can ***take*** souls maybe it can also find souls!

That's not something the Soultaker can do.
But have you ever tried it?
Well... no.

Soultaker, please help us find the soul of Mr. O'Shaughnessy.
It might help to have something of his. Or at least that he touched recently?
We aren't allowed any personal effects here at the Burrito Bucket.
It's a very professional establishment.
Oh! I know!
Are you okay?
I am victorious!

We'll see if this works.

Gi. Yu. Jin. Rei. Makoto. Meiyo. Chugi. Jisei.

In the name of Muramasa the maker, I command the whispers of the soul which touched this burrito to reunite with their true life!

WHOOOSH

Lead me to your true soul.
Aww, he's adorable.
POP

Is that a ghost?!
Is my boss—?
No, not a ghost—more like a soul remnant. Think of him as a wisp of the soul who last touched the burrito. I think.

Aww, wisp sounds so cute!
Maybe if trash-can burritos weren't involved.
My hope is that he will feel pulled to join the main soul. That will lead me to all the places Shane O'Shaughnessy would normally go.
Or wherever other remnants of him are the strongest.
Brilliant! I hope you're ready to watch a *lot* of paperwork.
Well, that's if it works. The Soultaker is generally for taking souls, not reuniting them.

I'm sure it'll work.
Whatever gets me closer to finding my father. Even if it's actual garbage food.

Who could have ever guessed conjuring a baby ghost soul would be so boring?
Uuggghhhhh.

There are plenty of paths for us each to follow. You go and see if you can find Zatanna's father. I'll stay and track the wisp.

Great idea! I'll scan the skies! I need to stretch.

Yes! Bumblebee, will you head back to the casino with me to see if there are any clues I missed?
Of course!

Green Lantern and I will search the boardwalk...for your father and Steve Trevor.

Good luck, Katana. I have a feeling you're in for the most boring evening of your life.
Seriously, sometimes I dump ice from the ice machine down the back of my shirt just to stay awake when he's talking to me.
I have faced greater trials.

Just in case.

This can't be all he does. Can you hear me? Where does he go **after** the paperwork?!

Sigh.

Well, I guess we'll see if water does the trick.

Ahhh! I'm awake! Wow, that is cold!

Seriously?! You're leaving now?

CLEANERS

May I help you?
Me? Oh no, thank you. He's the one who—
Oh right. He doesn't speak.
"He" who?

I am here for a very important task. To pick up the dry cleaning for Mr. Shane O'Shaughnessy.
Slip, please.

Slip?
The receipt? To pick up the clothing? The one he certainly would have given you before sending you here?

chapter seven

Oh, I must have...thrown it away with my burrito wrapper?
Was that before or after you fell in the river?

Oh, I am so sorry about that. Do you have some towels? I am happy to clean it up.

Just tell O'Shaughnessy next time I'm charging double.
The glitter and sequins get everywhere.
This can't be right. He's way too boring for—

Are you sure Shane sent you?
I am... sure...that... I am here on his behalf?

Diana can't be mad at me. Technically that was the truth.
Now, what did Mr. O'Shaughnessy do with *this?*

And now for the tenth installment of the docuseries Watching Paint Dry. Today's color is eggshell.
Really? He needs green sequins for this?!
BZZZ! BZZZ! BZZZ!
Wonder Woman, did you find Mr. Zatara, or anyone?

No one. Green Lantern called it a town of ghosts, but truly there is nothing spectral here. Nothing, not even a whole vase.
Ancient Greek pottery... at the boardwalk?

I have been unable to locate a single soul. I really am losing my edge, Katana.

You're not. I promise you, Diana of Themyscira, if anyone can figure out what is happening, it's you. Just trust your gut.

My guts are inside my body. I am unsure how to ask them, but I am confident they would not lie to me.
Exactly.

And my gut says there is more to Mr. O'Shaughnessy than watching paint dry.

SLICE!

Okay, you are my clue here.

You like this, huh, buddy? Show me where a man who loves spreadsheets and documentaries on the color beige wears green sequins.

MALLORY O'MADDEN'S
A corned beef and cabbage restaurant?! It's not even open this late!

Irish Fest Dance-Off!
Oh, thank goodness you're here! We're short a dancer.
What? Oh no—I don't dance.

Siobhan found a new dancer!
Hooray!
My name's Katana and I'm no dancer.

I'm just here looking for someone, actually. Shane O'Shaughnessy.
Yeah, so are we.

How dare he skip our final Dance-Off rehearsal? Not even the step champion five years running gets to miss practice!
Champion? Mr. O'Shaughnessy?

Oh yeah, he's the best. But suddenly I guess that means he's too good to show up.
I suspect foul play.
So do I! Do you have a suspect?

Lena Luthor may look like an innocent child, but I wouldn't put it past her to wipe out the competition.
Nor would I.

You know, the best way to investigate would be to stay near her...on the dance floor.

Besides, a costume that amazing is meant for fancy footwork.
I guess, sword fighting is like a dance...

So it's settled!
I'll teach you the steps. Just don't move your upper body at all. The key is rigidity and discipline.

Oh, I love rigidity and discipline! Diana is going to be so envious she missed this!

Oh how lovely!
They might take home the pot of gold even without Shane!
TAP
TAP
TAP
SLIP
Ooops! Sorry, I dropped my lollipop.
Oh you poor, sweet lass.
You did that on purpose.
I'll do whatever it takes to win.

So will I.
Keep stepping!
Yes! May the road rise to meet us!
May the wind be at our back!
Wow, dancing on *air!*

We have our winners! The Stepping Shanes!
Uhhhh...call us the Kicking Katanas!

Tell me what you did with Mr. O'Shaughnessy.
What I did?! Clearly he replaced himself with a ringer.

You didn't kidnap Mr. O'Shaughnessy?
I'm a Luthor. If I had some sort of master plan, I'd be gloating about it.
If Lena didn't kidnap Mr. O'Shaughnessy, why did you bring me here, wisp?

AHHHHH!!

The lights?!

THWANG

Roan?! Where's Roan?
Where's Lena?

A lot of dancers are missing.

The culprit was here.

chapter eight

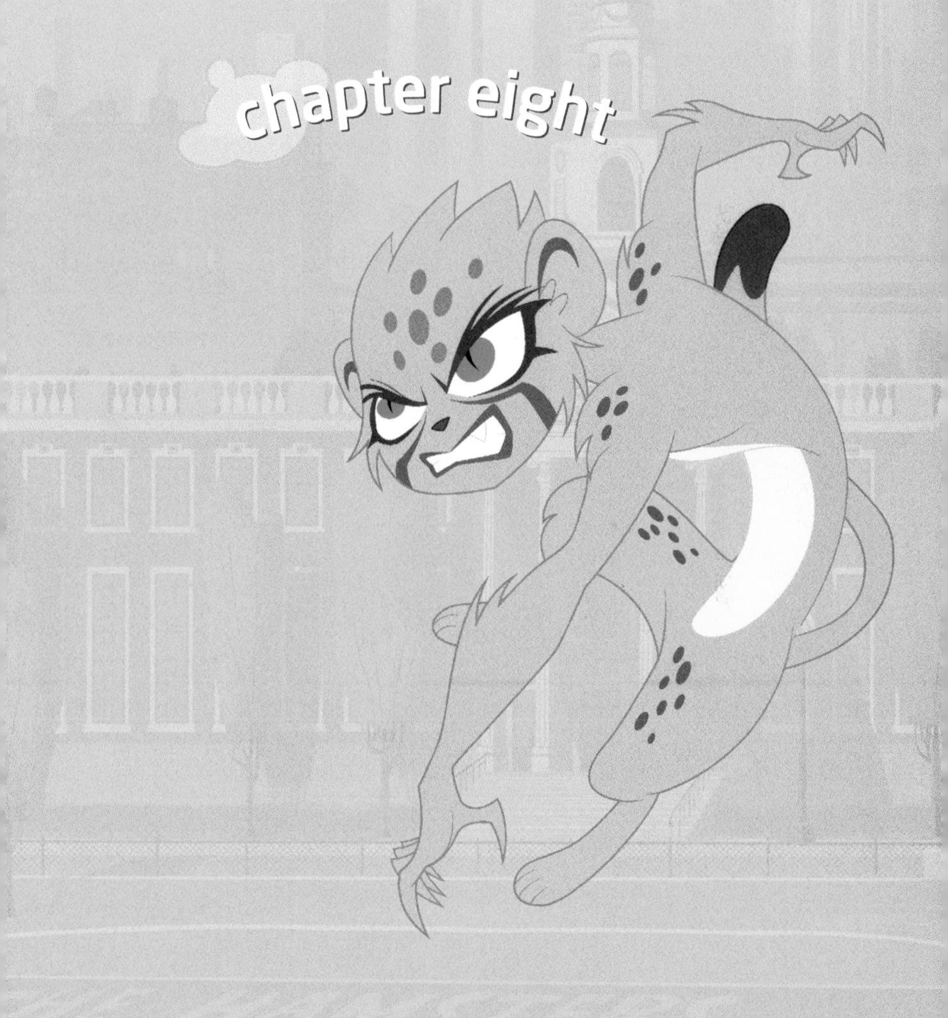

I swear, if this is a line-dancing contest I will just give you to Lena Luthor myself...after I find her. And...you.

You told me we'd win!
Yeah, well, there were unexpected complications.

But nothing I can't fix with a little help.

Where's Lena? You can't possibly expect either one of us to help you now.
Oh, you won't have a choice.

AHHHHHHHH!
Ahahahaha!
My coalition of Cheetahs grows!

Growl!
Gasp!
Don't worry.
I can handle a lot more than two angry Cheetahs.
It is time to prowl! Join me, sisters!
GROWL!
SNARL!
PURRRR!
GRRRRR
Okay, maybe not that many.

Now that I have enough of you, the true work will begin. We'll raid every museum. Take every artifact...

Though of course, with so many of us...some of us are bound to get caught.

But that's okay. I'm worth it. Which is why *you* will be going to the casino tonight.
To create a distraction.

I need to warn the rest of the Super Hero Girls.

Come on, wisp. You look like a little glowing cat toy and I have no idea what the rules are for a soul remnant. Can you be killed?

Are you even alive?

THWMP!
Fur.
Sigh.
GRRRRRRRRR.
CLANG!

No! Watch out, wisp!

Well, that answers the question about if you can be killed.

Ha! Rigidity and discipline!

Stop her!

You may want to hold on, little wisp.

THUNK

Where is she?
It doesn't matter. Let's get to the casino.

I've got to tell Zatanna!

He's not in here.
Not in here, either.
BZZz
TATSU

Wohs em ym dad!

That should have shown me where he was no matter what.
Do you think that means he's here?

BZZZ
TATSU
I wish.

He's not in there either, but those rabbits might need a lesson on how carrots are different than bumblebees.

One last try, then we can go home for the night.

Evig em ym dad!

Zatanna! It's working!
I think so!

Uh... Dad?

METROPOLIS HIGH SCHOOL

chapter nine

THE
AZING ZATARAS
Okay, we'll try Wonder Woman.

DIANA

Bob Hall
Beth Abe
Dixie Jones
Missing
DAVID WEST
SUZIE BECK
LYLE SMALL
Green Lantern, over here!

Missing
MICHAEL WILLIAMS
LIAM SMITH
Steve? Steve Trevor? Are you there?
...I just don't understand what I am overlooking.
BZZ BZZ BZZ

Tatsu?

A coalition?! To the casino? Call Supergirl and Batgirl. Green Lantern and I will be there in the split of a lick.
It's *lickety split*...but no one really says that anymore so maybe just tell her we're on our way.

We've got to go!

GRRROOOWWWLLL!

It looks like Cheetah arrived before us. Hurry, Super Hero Girls!
Whoa, so this is what a coalition of Cheetahs looks like.
When I'm finished it will be more like a cat-astrophe!
Let us use screws to place our courage on sticks!
Screw our courage to the sticking place?
Also that.
Eseht stac od ton dnal no rieht teef!
EXIT

You girls are just in time!

Leave Bumblebee alone.

Nice footwork, Katana!
I learned some new moves.

You must show them to me when we train later.
Gladly.
RAAAWWWWRRR

See? I told you Cheetahs never prosper.
Oh, lately I feel like Cheetah has been very prosperous, much to my disappointment with myself.

It's just a pun, Wonder Woman.

Batgirl is right. You're doing amazing.

That is for my father.

Nettik!
And that's for destroying our set!

And that's because I'm annoyed.
CLANG!
CLANG!
TWANG!

You're cornered, Cheetah. Tell your coalition to back off.

You heard Wonder Woman.
RAAAWWWWRRR

The Cheetahs are fleeing.

I can still catch them!
It is no use.

Cheetah bested me again. I am not sure I am fit to be your leader.
Of course you are! This isn't you. This is something... else.

Batgirl is right. I used all my magic to try to summon my father and instead a Cheetah clone jumped out of a hat.
We're dealing with something very powerful.

EXIT
And I don't think this was even the real target.

The museums.

There are much better places to rob if you're gonna go through all this for a distraction.
But not if you want ancient artifacts that contain ancient powers.

Sounds like it is time for a trip to the library!
Yes! We shall go first thing to eat worms with the morning birds!
Ugggggghhh My least favorite kind of bird.

She had some kind of mask in her hand.
More Batman-style or a full Halloween deal?

Neither. It looked...almost like stone? I can't find anything in any of these books about stone masks.

THE MASK OF DOLOS!

The what?!

DOLOS
The Greek God of Trickery
I learned about it on Themyscira. It's a magical totem.

I told you it was magic!
Let's go get a mask!

Back to the Natural History Museum!
SHHHHH!
Terribly sorry!
INFORMATION

Truly, we deeply respect library etiquette.
Just. Leave.

Now! Back to the Natural History Museum.

chapter ten

We're too late.
All the hard work we did to save this place and it's ruined...
But we didn't save it. She got exactly what she wanted the last time she came here...I really have lost my touch.
We wouldn't know what we were up against without your knowledge, Wonder Woman.
And now that we do, let's go find a mask.
DOLOS The Greek God of Trickery
Perhaps we could take a few moments to repair the irreplaceable artifacts?

Oh, allow me. Although I'm better at breaking a leg!
Oh no, whose leg have you broken?
Only on stage, darling.

Llup flesruoy rehtegot!

Let's show the Super Hero Girls to Cheetah's lair...well, all the Cheetahs' lair now, I guess.

We will be outnumbered.
Yes, which is why we need a plan...from our leader.

Luckily strategizing is my second-favorite hobby... right after training. Let us attach our heads to one another.
Put our heads together?
Yes!

First we shall need a distraction.
There are at least twenty Cheetahs in there.
Okay, several distractions.

"Supergirl will go in first and take the first three at the door..."
"Oh come on! I can take way more than three!"

"Of course, I would never want to underestimate your strengths. Supergirl will take on the first six at the door.

"Then Zatanna will create a distraction to lure more Cheetahs away from their lair."
Noitatimi yrettop!

Priceless relics!

"Which, of course...

"...will be a trap."
GRRRRRRRR...
Gotcha!

"Katana will take on the rest of the Cheetahs...

"And push them into a room...

"Which Batgirl will rig with a lock."
"Not just any lock! An electric lock sure to zap any ideas of escape right out of them."

Yelp!
"See?"

ZAPPPPPPP
"Fine...which Batgirl will rig with an electric lock.

"And I...
"I will face the real Cheetah."
Grrrr
You'll have to do better than that.

You're quite the gymnast.

I'm better.
You're right.

Mwahahahaha!
Sic her, girls!

Girls? Where's my coalition?
You may be a better gymnast...
I'm a better leader.

I'll be taking this.

NOOOOOOOOOO!

We got it!
Karen, thank you for getting it away from Cheetah. I am very impressed.
I guess all that training really was good for something.

I told you that you hadn't lost your edge, Diana.
Tatsu is right. You're an amazing leader.

Well, we haven't achieved victory yet. There are people trapped in this mask who need to be released.

Here's hoping this mask works like a burrito.

Gi. Yu. Jin. Rei. Makoto. Meiyo. Chugi. Jisei.

In the name of Muramasa the maker, I command the souls trapped inside this mask to be released!

Wait for it...wait for it...

Well, that was a bust.

Come on!
Esaeler Meht!

It's no use. I'm never gonna see my dad again.

Don't say that, Zee. We're not done. We'll figure it out.
Yes, of course we will. Right, Diana?

Of course we will!

chapter eleven

HISTORY OF MAGIC
MYTHS and LEGENDS
MASKS and MYSTERIES
GREEK MYTHS
CAT-TASTROPHES

Diana.

Oh, I am so sorry. Was I turning pages too loudly?
No, we're closing. You've been here for 12 hours.

Right. Well, what's the maximum number of books you allow someone to check out?
LEGEND OF DOLOS

MYTHS and LEGENDS
CAT-TASTROPHES
GREEK MYTHS
HISTORY OF MAGIC
MASKS and MYSTERIES
LEGEND OF DOLOS

Who's there?

Please just give me a moment to put my books down. They belong to the library.

I will not allow them to be injured!
Ha ha ha! Oh Diana.

It's just me.
When you didn't return for hours, I got worried.

And when you even missed training, I got *really* worried.
GREEK GODS

Are you okay?

I do not want to let everyone down. People we care about are gone.
I thought I had the answer and I do not.

Failure just means that you have tried something and can cross it off the list of possible solutions.
Wow, that is a terrific approach.

I like to think so. Shall we try to cross off some more?

Let us be failures!

Where are the people you've taken? Tell me the truth.

I'm gonna monitor it for signs of life!

The mask has no heartbeat!

ancient Greek incantations
old spells
give it a glass of water
take it for a nice walk
ask mask to tell the
scan mask for scientific signs of life

Maybe I can draw them out!

Are souls even magnetic?
There are no bad ideas!

Ahhhhhh! Ooof!
But there are dangerous ones.

Sorry, Bumblebee.
I wish I could say this was the first time I've been in a fight with a dessert spoon but it's not.

It's time to try things my way.

Whoa whoa whoa!
Ahhh, Supergirl. What if you hurt them?!

Eh, it seems okay. Cross another one off the list, Katana.

How many successful failures do we have?
We're on 472.

That is good, but not good enough!

Poor daddy, all this time trapped in there.
He's really not that good in masks.
Once for Halloween I went as Morgaine le Fey and he was my dragon and he only lasted in the mask for like ten minutes...

This is a totally different situation. It doesn't even seem like anyone is in the mask anyway!

Which on second thought may not be entirely reassuring.

We'll have to make more attempts with the mask later. There's been another break-in.

Where?
A construction site across town.

Why would someone rob a construction site? Is there a tool shortage?

Actually, if it's the Lexcorp parking lot dig, they accidentally uncovered a ton of ancient artifacts!
I bet Lex is thrilled.
And I bet Cheetah is intrigued. Super Hero Girls, let us engage in the haste making!

Wow, this really is a treasure trove of antiquities. I feel so at home.
The Super Hero Girls! Thank goodness. We're overrun with Cheetahs! There are just so many Cheetahs.
Did you know that's called a coalition?
Batgirl, this is not the time for facts of fun! Don't worry, construction person, we are here to help!

I sure hope so because I have no idea how we're gonna explain this to Mr. Luthor.

THWAP
GRRRRR...

Place these somewhere safe... and place yourself somewhere safe as well.
Sure thing.

Let's get these Cheetahs into captivity!
While I am generally against caging wild animals, this is a worthy exception.

GRRROWL
Supergirl, could you lend me a hand...or a breath?
SWOOSH!
Today's forecast is windy with a chance of bats!
Thank you, Batgirl!
Grrr...
Walced!
POOF!
Thanks, Zatanna!
Don't worry. I've got your back!

chapter twelve

CLANG!
THWUNK!
GROWWWL!
HISSS!
Eat stingers!

Hcnul ot og!
GRRRRRR!
Hurry! Get to safety!

AHHH!
Help!
AHHHHH!
Go quickly.
AHHHHH!
TWACK!
CRASH!
AHHHHHH!

You won't get away from me this time, Cheetah. I know the real you!

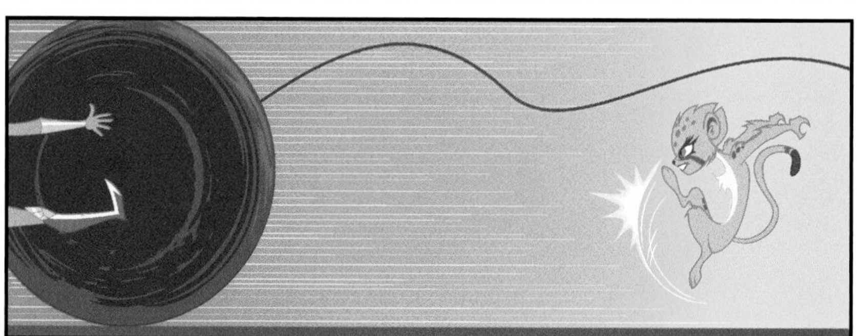

Ooooof.
Coalition, hold her down!
THUNK!
Let's **cement** your place in history.

Wonder Woman, do you need help?
No. I've got it. I just wish this Cheetah didn't have such intense burrito breath.
Wait...
Hissss!
SNIFF

GRRROWL!
Katana! Your sword!

This Cheetah has burrito breath! Huzzah!
They were never inside the mask. The mask just obscured their true identity!
SNIFF
Gi. Yu. Jin. Rei. Makoto. Meiyo. Chugi. Jisei.

In the name of Muramasa the maker, I command the soul trapped inside this fake Cheetah to be released!

Bring me as many Cheetahs as you can find.

What...
what happened?
Where am I?
Saved
by your own
halitosis! Isn't it
wonderful?!
You're okay.
Just go home, eat
some soup, and...
enjoy your dry
cleaning.
I...my breath?
My dry cleaning?!

Zatanna, summon
your father.
I've tried
that so many
times!

Just trust
me.

S'yddad Irig!
See? It never works. Every time I try to find my dad, I just end up covered in Cheetahs.
Yes, exactly!
Daddy!
Um, err...so good to see you, Mr. Zatara!
Good to have you back, Garth!
Thanks, Bumblebee!

You! I should have known.

Actually, Katana saved you.

You're lucky I have unfinished business with Cheetah.

Um, which one is the real Cheetah anyway?
We're still working that out.

It is this one. I'd know her anywhere.
Do you need help?
No, just keep releasing her captives.

I am crackling mad!
Wait, are we still in our truce, or—?
I don't know. I mean, on one hand you stood me up...on the other, it wasn't your fault.
The show is probably gonna be rescheduled. We could still—

Oh my gosh. It's Blundie!

Truce?
Absolutely!

Blundie, wait up! We're your biggest fans!
Can we have an autograph? Do you need a roadie? I'm great with lighting design!

Steve did not do the ghost!

Back to the matter at hand. Where is Cheetah?

She slipped away.
Oh no, she bested me again.

You know, I hate to contradict you... but you're wrong.

We have the mask and we figured out how to rescue and reunite everyone and that was all thanks to *YOU*, Wonder Woman.

Bumblebee is right. The things that really matter have been saved. You were able to see through the mask and tell us how to bring people together.
That's a very strong leader.

You're right! But I do still need to apologize to you.
I let doubt get in the way. I trained us so hard we were too tired to see the obvious.

Which is why to make it up to you...only four hours of training a day this week!
Four hours?!
I know right? That is not nearly enough. Is this a punishment?
Katana, you and Wonder Woman are peas in a pod.
I am no vegetable!

No, but you're a great friend. Which reminds me, I still have these gifts from Katana's first slumber party.
They're friendship necklaces. I made them myself. Because best friends stand by each other no matter what.
But they're also...
Smoke bombs for a clean getaway! Now go find Steve Trevor before he thinks you ghosted him.

Amanda Deibert is an award-winning television and comic book writer. Her work includes *DC Super Hero Girls, Teen Titans Go!, Wonder Woman '77, Sensation Comics Featuring Wonder Woman*, and a story in *Love Is Love* (a *New York Times* #1 bestseller) along with comics for IDW, Dark Horse, Bedside Press, and Storm King. She's written TV shows for CBS, Syfy, OWN, and Hulu, and for former vice president Al Gore's international climate broadcast, *24 Hours of Reality*.

Yancey Labat is the bestselling illustrator of the original *DC Super Hero Girls* graphic novel series. He got his start at Marvel Comics before moving on to illustrate children's books from *Hello Kitty* to *Peanuts* for Scholastic, as well as books for Chronicle Books, ABC Mouse, and others. His book *How Many Jelly Beans?* with writer Andrea Menotti won the 2013 Cook Prize for best STEM (Science, Technology, Education, Math) picture book from Bank Street College of Education.

Carrie Strachan is an award-awaiting colorist who has worked on *Hellblazer, Smallville: Season 11, MAD Magazine*, and *MAD Spy vs. Spy: An Explosive Celebration*. She currently lives in San Diego with her husband, Matt, where she's hard at work on more *DC Super Hero Girls*.

THE HEROIC CROSSOVER OF THE CENTURY!

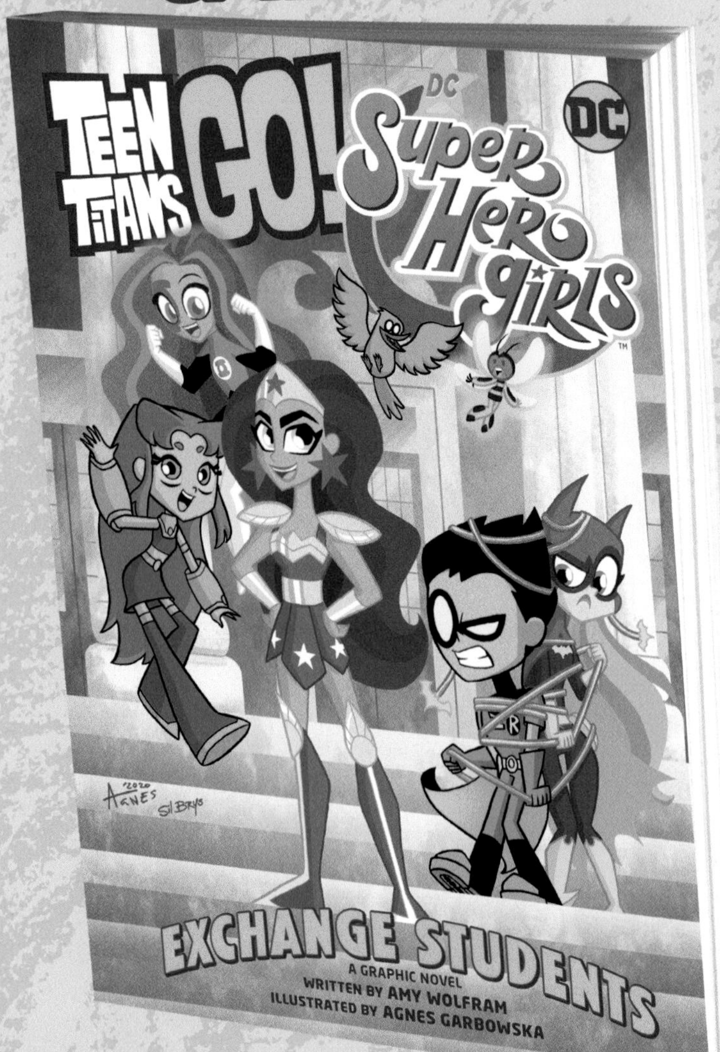

Starfire's evil sister has invaded Earth (again), but this time she's zapped herself to Metropolis High! It's up to the Teen Titans to follow her to this alternate Earth...and we'll see if the DC Super Hero Girls can stop their exchange student partners from causing bigger problems than the one they came to solve.

Amy Wolfram and **Agnes Garbowska** team up our teen troupes for an epic adventure!

CRASH
Don't mind me, just doing a little late-night shopping.

See you later!

Who was *that?*

Be sure to hit like and subscribe!

That was ba-na-nas.
What a cliffhanger!
Those Super Hero Girls are so cool, but even they didn't see that one coming.

You know, we'd never be surprised like that.

Wait. Go back.
What is it, Star?

What is my sister Blackfire doing in the Metropolis?

My sister has *broken out* of the prison of space again.

Why did Blackfire not come visit me or commit the crimes on *our* Earth?

Explain, Starfire. I thought we were just watching a show.

That was no show.
Somehow we were able to watch Livewire's channel from another *universe!*
We will have to go bring her the home.

Traveling between universes can be *dangerous.*

It's Metropolis. How dangerous can it be, Raven?

Did you not just say how the *cool* the Super Hero Girls are?

They are cool. But we can't just travel to another universe. If we ran into our other selves there it could create a rift in the whole multiversal space-time continuum and cause unknown repercussions.

We could really mess things up.